Raihanaty A. Jalil

# *Love, Faith & Numbers*

A Muslim Short Story Collection

First paperback edition June 2022

Author photograph by UWGY Entertainment
Edited by Emily Paull

ISBN 978-0-6452077-0-5 (paperback)

www.raihanaty.com

A catalogue record for this
work is available from the
National Library of Australia

# About the Author

Raihanaty A. Jalil was born in Malaysia to Indonesian parents and moved to Australia before the age of three. She is an avid Jane Austen reader who spent her childhood lost in her vivid imagination, playing out made-up characters in her backyard. She has been writing poetry and stories since Primary School, inspired by classic poets such as Elizabeth Barrett Browning and William Blake. She considers herself to be a jack of all trades and has led a very interesting life, taking on a variety of roles including poet, educator, entrepreneur, rapper and speaker. She believes that sharing her writing with others is akin to sharing a part of her soul.

Raihanaty has read her work during Perth Festival Writers Week, at The Wheeler Centre for the Digital Writers' Festival and has sat on the board for Centre for Stories. Raihanaty has facilitated poetry workshops at the Australian

Islamic College for Propel Youth Arts WA. Her creative non-fiction and short fiction has appeared in the anthologies, Wave After Wave and To Hold The Clouds (Centre for Stories, Australia).

# Contents

# Contents

# Arranged Introduction

There's a knock on the door. You should be nervous but you're not. It's just Ahmad. You still remember his thick-rimmed glasses, high-pitched voice, but the clincher? His obsession with Pokémon. Sure, you like anime too, but the point is, he's a dork. So why did you agree to this again?

"Zakia, he's here," Mum tells you as she enters.

"I know." Your eyes remain fixed in the mirror, adjusting your pastel pink hijab and straightening the white under-cap.

"Your father's talking to him in the living room. Come to the kitchen first and bring out the tea."

You groan. This has got to be a Bollywood cliché, but then again, bringing him tea is better than being like, "Hi, so yeah, here I am, your potential wife."

You sigh out loud. Why are you doing this again? Your phone pings and you remember—Minder, the Muslim version of Tinder. And that Sydney guy you matched with who flew across the country to see you, who told you almost every day, "I think this will work out." (At least *before* he met you face-to-face.)

You grimace, remembering his exact words in the car after picking him up from the airport, "You look different in person..."

*That's* why you agreed to this. If you're not married before the age of thirty, you'll expire, die a spinster.

Well, okay, maybe not. But kids. You really *really* want kids. You're reminded of this every time you visit Hafsa and her babies run to you, begging you to make paper planes again. You've already mapped it out. At least a year to enjoy married life, then a boy and a girl, two years apart. Close enough in age so they can grow together, but enough time between them to get better at the parenting thing.

"Zakia!" Mum hisses, holding the tray of tea.

"Sorry, I'm ready now."

You walk like you're learning to take your first steps—because of the tea. This is not good. What was Mum thinking suggesting the idea? Did she forget all your food-related disasters, dishes of all kinds somehow finding the floor? Worse, that wedding you helped out at, the cake entrusted to you that landed, splat, on the bitumen floor as you got out of the car. Thank God it wasn't *the* wedding cake, but still, the trauma.

"Eep!" You rebalance the two sets of gold-rimmed cups and saucers that only make an appearance once or twice a year—for Eid, the rare occasion you have visitors. The lounge room is in sight but you keep your eyes on the brown liquid that swishes from side to side like the waves at Scarborough Beach.

He's in your peripheral vision now but the tea, focus on landing the tea safely on the coffee table, you think. Phew, done, success!

You look up. Your eyes widen. This is not at all the Ahmad of your memories. But why are you surprised exactly when the last time you saw him was in Year 5 or 6?

You swallow, dart your eyes away—trying not to perv. Are you allowed to perv, though, seeing as he might end up your husband?

"I'll go see if your Mum needs any help with lunch," your father says, getting up.

You nod. Your cheeks heat up when Dad squeezes your shoulder, his grin stretching from ear to ear. He gives you a peck and leaves.

You sit on the couch across from Ahmad.

"Assalamu Alaikum," he says, his chocolate eyes smiling.

"Wa Alaikum Salam." You focus on his oval face, close-trimmed beard, lashes that are unfairly long and curly. (You're actually trying not to gawk at his broad shoulders, how his green

long-sleeved t-shirt clings to his defined muscles.)
You sigh. Crap, did he notice?

"You're beautiful," Ahmad says.

Your heart drums in your flushed ears. You
meet his warm gaze. "You're not so bad yourself."
Woah, did you just say that aloud?

He chuckles.

You distract yourself with some tea.

He follows suit, takes a sip and asks, "How was
your day?"

You shrug. "Oh, you know, *really* tough. Spent
all morning choosing something to wear."

He laughs again. "Well, it paid off."

Oh boy, you're not used to this forwardness
but, you like it. You reward him with a Colgate
smile.

"Were you nervous?" he asks as he turns his
half-empty cup.

"To be honest, not really. You were a bit of a
dork back in school," you say in a playful tone but
immediately clamp your mouth. What's gotten
into you? This is dangerous, how easy and
comfortable it is right now.

But Ahmad laughs even harder. "I've got contacts now."

"Oh, it wasn't just the glasses. Your oversized clothes—"

"Hand-me-downs," he interrupts.

"Fair enough. How about singing the Pokémon theme song *all* the time!"

This time, Ahmad is in hysterics. "Wow, you remember that?"

You give him a lop-sided grin. "Guess you made an impression?"

He casts you a teasing glance. "Hmm, maybe you liked me unconsciously all this time."

"Nah, not a chance."

He clutches his heart Bollywood style.

"Oh God, please don't," you say, but your cheeks ache from smiling so much.

Ahmad leans back into the leather two-seater and shakes his head.

You raise an eyebrow. "Something wrong?"

He sits forward and gives you a serious look. Slowly, he says, "Yes..."

You don't tear away your gaze but your stomach churns. Did you go too far? Did you show too much too soon—the mistake you made with *him*? The guy you met in uni who ghosted you after four months, your first love whose remnants still blotch the surface of your heart.

You grip the ceramic handle tighter. No, you remind yourself. It doesn't matter. You have to be authentic, one-hundred-per-cent you, take it or leave it. You're not going to lose yourself in the process this time.

You take a deep breath. In a measured tone, you ask, "What is it?"

Ahmad breaks into a teasing smile and gazes at you with warmth. "I'm in trouble."

# In the Green

If his voice had a colour, it would be black, contrasting his hard white features. His stern blue eyes bulged beneath his furrowed brows. "My name is Constable Williams," he said. "As you can see, I have two cameras that will capture every word you say. I've recorded your speed at 94. Why were you doing 94 in a 60 zone?"

Huh? 60 zone?

Zakia swallowed as she stared at his four eyes, two of them cameras suspended on each side of his helmet. "Uh... I... umm..." It was like his words, his accusation, reached her mind in slow motion, imposing time for her to conjure a response. "Err... I was... uh... daydreaming... sorry!"

A surprised look. "Oh." His features softened as he looked at her puss-in-boots gaze. "I'll just write you a ticket then..." His tone teetered on uncertainty. He turned towards his chequered motorcycle.

Zakia's heart knocked loudly against her chest. She gripped her steering wheel tighter, willing the cold plastic to absorb the tremors in her hands. She drove this route every day to work, had the speed limits memorised in her subconscious— clearly her downfall. She leaned back into her seat and sighed. Actually, no, she thought. The real culprit was daydreaming about Ahmad, their first introduction and how well their subsequent "Halal dates" in her living room had gone. His lazy brown eyes, his teasing smile, his broad shoulders... She shook her head. She was about to be hit with a huge fine, for goodness's sake!

Zakia stared at the rear-view mirror, growing more anxious the longer the officer took. A deep intake of breath when he returned to her open window.

He peeled off the white and blue layers from the poisonous tri-toned sandwich. "It's quite a hefty fine," he said gently, avoiding direct eye contact.

"How much?"

"$800 and six demerit points." He handed her the sheets. "It's because of roadworks," he added quietly then gave her a moment to absorb it all. There was an unkind benevolence in his silence. "You can pay it in person at any post office."

"Okay," Zakia said, staring at the figure. She traced the three digits with her eyes. The handwriting looked tired, overworked, almost illegible—almost. Zakia wished she could somehow unsee her name, her licence number or at least one zero.

She turned her attention back to the officer. "Sorry, I missed your name?"

His jawline hardened and his authoritative tone returned. "Constable Williams. It's written there on the fine."

"I'm Zakia," she said with a smile. "Thank you. Hope you have a good day."

A bewildered look. "Oh." He gave her an uncertain smile. "Thanks..." He took a step back as she wound her window up.

As Zakia pulled back out onto the freeway, eyes constantly darting back and forth to the speedometer, she raised an eyebrow at herself in the rear-view mirror. Why did she thank him exactly?

Somewhere in her subconscious, a memory tugged. Details hazy. An issue with her bank? Yes, a problem with the account she had called customer support about. Not once, multiple times on consecutive days. It was all very frustrating but she had remained cool and firm while treating the staff with kindness. Not only was her issue resolved, they had credited her twenty bucks as an appeasement. $20—a nice meal, a night out at the cinema.

Maybe it was wishful thinking but she believed treating people well, especially in frustrating situations, attracted good karma. Or maybe it was since she had started working in retail—on

...e receiving end of disgruntled customers—that he'd grown a new layer of empathy.

Zakia glanced at the time on the dashboard and grimaced, suddenly realising she should have started work five minutes ago. She looked at the phone perched against the air vent, wondering if she dared to pick it up and use it to call in.

No, don't even think about it, she said to her reflection, narrowing her brows. She'd already lost $800 and six points today.

$800—a new mobile phone, return tickets overseas, a designer handbag... it was so painful.

Zakia sighed again.

Everything happens for a reason, she thought.

Yeah, you need to stop speeding, came another voice in her head—her Mum's.

But no, there had to be more to it.

Car... It must be car-related. What's happened relating to her car?

Zakia's eyes lit up: the accident!

She turned to the passenger seat—her handbag, her notebook—but jerked her attention back to the road.

Zakia drove up the ramp that led to the designated staff parking for Garden City Shopping Centre. She was now half an hour late, so what were another few minutes?

She flipped through her journal, eyes skimming the top of each lined page until she found the heading.

*Money.*

*Car accident. Insurance quote: $3000 to fix damage. Car value: $1000–2000. Proposed payout: $1500. Actual cost to fix (mates rates): $500. Profit: $1000.*

She fished for a pen from her bag, scrawled the date and added *Speeding fine: $800. Balance to date = $1000 – $800 = $200 profit.*

Her lips curved upwards. She shoved the book back in her bag and bounced into work.

She slowed her steps at the sight of her manager and bent her head.

"Kelly," she said meekly. "I'm so sorry I'm late. Got stopped by the police for speeding. Didn't want to risk another fine calling you..."

"Oh no, Zakia, that's crap! How much you get done for?"

"$800 and six demerits."

"$800! That's crazy!"

Zakia shrugged. "Yeah, it sucks, but my bad for daydreaming... And thankfully, I'm still ahead."

Kelly frowned. "Ahead?"

Zakia smothered a smile. "Long story," she said, glancing at her watch. "Tell you later."

"I'm dying to see that movie! Heard it was really good."

Zakia grinned at Bianca while taking the last sip of her mocha. "Yeah, we should watch it soon though. People keep posting about it on Facebook. I'm scared of spoilers!"

"You're right," Bianca said, leaning forward. "How about next weekend?"

Zakia tapped and swiped her phone's display and noticed Ahmad was due to visit on Saturday.

"What are you smiling about, Zee?" Bianca interrupted.

Zakia's cheeks flushed. "Err... a funny reminder popped up," she said without meeting the eye of her long-time high school friend. She wasn't ready to tell Bianca about Ahmad, not until things were more concrete. Bianca knew about all her previous crushes and *him*. It was too tiring, the thought of being asked for updates, as well-meaning as their intent may be.

When it may not even work out, she thought as she pushed the painful image of her ex from her mind. She turned back to Bianca and ignored her sceptical expression. "I can do Sunday afternoon," she said.

"Done!"

They both stood up, their wooden chairs groaning against the varnished floorboards.

"Text you the day before to confirm the time?" Zakia asked.

"Sounds good."

Zakia shielded herself from the slap of cold air, pulling her fluffy coat tighter. Her phone vibrated in her pocket. *Speeding fine due*, it reminded her. She wrinkled her nose. She hated, *hated*, losing money, but at least she was in the green.

She approached her beat-up Toyota Corolla and her heart sank. A small piece of paper fastened to the windscreen-wiper waved back and forth like a spoilt child.

"Please let it be a flyer..." She chanted the words under her breath as if they could manifest into her reality.

*City of Perth*, it greeted in her favourite colour. Her shoulders slumped. She glanced down the narrow page with bated breath.

"Phew!"

Only $60. Still in the green.

# Nikah

Clothes everywhere. Literally. Long, short, striped, plain, colours. Every colour in the bubblegum paddle-pop.

"Oh my God!" Bianca said. "What does modest even mean?"

She picked up the red dress for the seventh time and held it against her body. Couldn't Zakia have given her more specific guidelines?

*Modest attire*, the invitation had said. Should she google modest? Oh, for God's sake, she knew what the word meant. Skin, that's what modesty was about, right? Less skin.

Bianca inspected the long sleeves of her dress whose length reached the floor. It did have a low V-neck but if she wore a body-top underneath it might be all right... Plus, she would be covering her hair.

And yet, weren't certain colours considered immodest in some cultures? Red was a very bold colour. What if she arrived at the mosque and everyone was dressed in black while she stood out like Father Christmas? What if they banned her from attending because of how offensive she looked?

"Zakia! Seriously, I'm going to kill you," she said aloud as she tossed aside the garment.

Bianca took a deep breath. Was black the safest bet? She didn't want to look like she was in mourning—although she was a bit uneasy about this whole thing.

I can't believe I'm even allowing myself to think this! No, I'm not being open-minded, she argued. Yet perhaps it was the fact that Zakia hadn't had the best history with men, picking morons who barely gave her a chance, one scarring her deeply after ghosting her. Or maybe it was Bianca's work in the community sector, having seen many domestic violence cases that made her anxious.

As for what to wear, Muslims weren't monsters. Surely, they'd cut her some slack if she wasn't dressed "perfectly".

"Oh!" She said as an idea popped into her head. She didn't own a scarf but that beach sarong could suffice.

*"Where do you get your scarfs from, Zee? They're so pretty!" she had asked Zakia once.*

*Zakia had shrugged. "Just the normal shops. There are Muslim women's clothing stores. But to be honest, they're much more expensive than, like, sarongs you find at Kmart or Myer."*

One last glance in the mirror. The off-white material cascaded over her shoulders. She slung one end across her body to cover her décolletage. "God, what was I thinking! I look even more like Santa!" she said as she stared at her red-white combo. Her phone pinged with a calendar reminder that it was time to leave. Too late to change. She grabbed some matching white heels and click-clacked out the door.

"Stace, that's such a good idea," Bianca said in a hush. They both sat on their knees in the cramped space of multi-coloured bodies. "I wish I'd thought of dressy pants... although I'm feeling very underdressed."

"Tell me about it!" Stacey said in equal hushed tones. She returned the smile of the middle-aged lady sitting next to her who was wearing a dress that looked like it had been hand-beaded from head to toe. "I was going to call—"

"Ooh, there she is," Bianca said, motioning with her head to the front of the small room.

"Wow..."

Zakia's white dress was made of two pieces, embroidered with silver flowers at the sleeves and down the skirt. The matching white lace scarf fell in ripples around her shoulders. She sat on her knees, head bent, facing the side of the room.

Bianca lifted her head and turned left and right. Where was the groom? Yes, it was a room full of only women but how did her bestie get married without her man? A green curtain separated the women's section from the men's, so could he be on the other side? Did she get to see him at all, though?

It was unsettling to Bianca, not having met the guy. It had all happened so fast—too fast. I mean, three months. Can you know a person well enough to marry them in three months?

*"Sit down,"* Zakia had said when she'd visited her place for a movie night in.

*"You're making me nervous, Zee. What is it?"*

*"It's exciting, I promise. But you need to sit down for this."*

*A million thoughts had run through Bianca's head, like did her bestie get a new job? Oh no, not overseas! Was she leaving the country?*

*But nothing prepared her for Zakia's next words.*

*"I've met someone... and we're getting married next week."*

*"What!" Bianca nearly slipped off the edge of Zakia's bed. "How? When? What?"*

*Zakia laughed until she was shaking and tears pooled in her eyes.*

*"Oh my God, Zee! Spill already!!"*

*"Okay, okay! We met through family. We actually went to the same Muslim Primary School but he was a dork back then."* She paused, her eyes growing shy. *"He's not a dork anymore..."*

*It was Bianca's turn to laugh. "When did this all happen? How long have you been talking? How come you kept this a secret from me!!"*

"Mabrook!" Applause broke Bianca's stream of consciousness, bringing her back to the reality of the small but peaceful place. She turned to Stacey perplexed, who shrugged. They looked around at what seemed like congratulatory faces but... She'd been staring at Zakia the whole time. She was sure Zakia hadn't uttered a word, so what was going on?

Kind chocolate eyes met Bianca's. Bianca smiled.

"The Nikah is done," the lady said.

Bianca raised an eyebrow.

"They're officially married." The woman beamed with excitement.

"Oh!" Bianca forced another grin to hide her shock and confusion. "That's wonderful!" she said unconvincingly. But the groom... where was he? "Stace, I zoned out... Did Zee..."

Stacey shook her head. "I didn't see her say anything either," she said in a whisper. "It's probably just how they do things?"

Bianca bit her tongue. She fought back the stupid images from movies she'd, unfortunately, watched about forced arranged marriages. But that was far from what Zakia was experiencing, she was sure, remembering Zakia's excitement when she shared the news. She looked at Zakia's face. Her look was demure. Maybe that was a cultural thing as well, to not look exuberant? Or was it?

Bianca let out a breath. Her head ached from her conflicting emotions. The perils of working with domestic violence victims, she thought. If they could just see the guy, see them together, maybe it would—

"Bianca, I think we're allowed to congratulate her," Stacey said.

One person after another approached Zakia, hugging then kissing her on each cheek multiple times. Most of the women seemed to do two kisses although the odd few went as much as four. There were chuckles when a woman assumed the wrong number and words were exchanged to confirm an agreed figure.

Bianca and Stacey weaved their way closer and finally caught their friend's eye.

"Oh my God, you're here!" Zakia said, throwing her arms around each and squeezing them tight.

"Of course! We wouldn't miss this, hun!" Stacey said.

Zakia laughed. "I'm so glad you could make it. So, what did you think?"

"It's... fascinating," Bianca said. "Does the..." She trailed off. Should she ask? Would it be offensive? Would it show her ignorance? Her eyes darted behind them at the queue of bodies waiting their turn.

Stacey followed Bianca's eyes then said. "We're so happy for you, hun! We better let the next person get to you."

Zakia pulled them into another hug. "Thanks so much, guys! It means a lot having you here. We have to catch up when I'm back from our honeymoon. Actually, I probably need a bit of time to get used to my new life..."

Bianca squeezed Zakia's shoulder. "Take your time, Zee. We're not going anywhere."

Bianca and Stacey lingered outside the cream building. A striking geometric pattern adorned its distinctive minaret. Still no sign of the dude. Maybe the groom didn't even make an appearance at a Muslim wedding?

Men filed out of another entrance, their clothing plainer. She turned to Stacey. "Does Zakia get to see her man, do you think?"

"You're asking me?"

Bianca laughed then immediately sighed.

"Should we ask someone?" Stacey said.

Bianca wrinkled her nose. "Is it okay to ask, though? I mean, are we putting Western expectations on a Muslim wedding?"

Stacey looked thoughtful. "Good point... But surely there's no harm in asking a polite question."

"I suppose..."

"I don't mind asking," Stacey said, looking around, trying to catch the eye of one of the women near her.

Bianca hung back, turning to check the car park. It didn't look like people were leaving.

"Oh, I think something's happening."

Bianca followed Stacey's eyes. An entourage of men all dressed in white robes moved with purpose. The scattered women around them stepped aside. Phones left handbags and were positioned, ready for whatever was about to happen.

Bianca and Stacey approached the growing crowd. A few heads turned and glanced at their attempts at modest attire. Warm smiling faces beckoned them nearer and space was made for them.

"Do you think one of them is the groom?" Bianca asked Stacey quietly.

"Must be."

Yet none of the men stood out. They were of different ages. One or two were dressed in a suit and tie. But most were wearing that long white dress you saw Arab Sheikhs wear on TV. Maybe look for silver? Zakia had silver in her dress, so could the guy be colour-coordinated with her?

"Ooh, she's coming out!"

Bianca jerked her head, her eyes falling on her friend who slipped her henna-painted feet into silver heels. Zakia looked into the group of men, a shy smile spreading across her features. A tall guy emerged, his face a beacon of excitement and pleasure. A few steps on either side before he took her hand and pulled her into an embrace. He whispered something in her ear that made her blush and hugged her again.

Bianca blinked away the emotion that pooled in her eyes and let out a relieved breath. Her best friend was going to be okay.

# Relationship Maths

A hmad, I miss you. Call me when you're on your break.

One minute later.

*What are you up to?*

Five minutes later.

*Shouldn't it be your lunchtime now? Call me please.*

Ten minutes later.

*Can't you reply with at least an acknowledgment? Just one emoji. Is that so hard?*

Thirty minutes later.

*Baby, are you okay? Did something happen at work? Not hearing from you is making me stress... Please please reply.*

*Busy.*

Zakia stared at the four-letter word. Relief—always her first feeling. But then came annoyance.

"Ugh!!!" She threw her phone onto their bed. For God's sake, what was wrong with men? She was patient for over half an hour. Yet, was she being unreasonable?

She shook her head. No, *he* was being inconsiderate.

He knows how much I *hate* silence! Zakia thought. Why does he keep doing this to me?

She stared at the black display that coaxed her to give him a piece of her mind. Her hand moved an inch closer but she threw herself on his side of the bed and sighed out loud.

I can't keep going through this.

She turned on her side. Looked around her room for some distraction. A pile of unread books. Washing yet to be put away. Her laptop.

Her eyes lit up. Budgeting, she thought. That usually injected her with excitement.

Zakia groaned as she forced her body up and sought her bag. She pulled out her purse made of red saffiano-leather, its signature "O" glimmering in gold. Remembering it was Ahmad's one-year anniversary gift, annoyance brewed again.

Budgeting, budgeting, budgeting.

She unfastened the magnetic buckle that held together every receipt from the past few days. One by one, the rectangle sandwich thinned. She stacked the pieces of paper into rough piles based on category: petrol, groceries, splurge, Sadaqah. That last pile from donations made her feel good—the only investment with guaranteed returns since God was the broker.

Zakia opened her banking app. Figures of each pile added, she swiped to move money between her five savings accounts. She punched in the numbers and refreshed the page to see the updated balances.

*Allahu Akbar, Allahu Akbar!*

Her phone reverberated the call to prayer. Salah time. Exactly what she needed.

She headed to the bathroom. Toilet first. Then Wudhu.

The not-yet-warm water woke her mind as the liquid passed over her hands, face, arms and eventually feet. She dried the excess with her red towel that touched his petrol-green one. His towel that wouldn't be used for another week...

Bloody hell. Get out of my head!

Three deep breaths.

Yaa Haleem, Yaa Haleem, Yaa Haleem, she chanted in her mind.

Oh, Allah, help me, she prayed with closed eyes before returning to her room—their room.

Zakia lay the machine-woven Sajadah with the picture of the Ka'bah on the varnished floor. She raised her hands to her shoulders, uttering the words she'd learnt in her childhood even before the English alphabet. She didn't concentrate as consistently as she should, but today, her mind yearned for peace and clarity.

Her movements were slow into each posture—Qiyam, Ruku', Sajdah, Jalsah. She focussed her eyes on the same spot. Her lips moved, repeating words of praise, gratitude and prayer in an inaudible hush. When she concluded the four sets with Salam to the angel on each shoulder who recorded her good and bad deeds, she remained seated. She loved this moment after every Salah—

hated being stripped of this state of high in the stolen prayers at work in the storage room while her colleagues ate lunch. Sometimes she fed her stomach first before she fed her spirit so the former could not encroach on the needs of the latter.

"Alhamdulillah," Zakia chanted quietly as the beginnings of an idea took shape in her mind.

She folded her prayer attire and mat. She returned to the bed with her laptop and created a new spreadsheet.

*Ahmad Experiment*, she typed as the table heading, then created seven columns: *Hypothesis, Action, Start Date, End Date, Period (days), Results and Conclusion*.

Zakia straightened her back, the buzz of excitement surging through her shoulders. She filled in the columns.

*Hypothesis: Ahmad will be more responsive to my messages if I contact him less*

*Action: For one week, I will not initiate contact*

*Start Date: Fri 16 September*

"Ahmad, I turn into a crazy version of myself in long silences. It's not your fault. It's because of my ex—" Zakia's voice faltered. She looked away. She swallowed the ache that always began in her throat. She blinked several times until the wetness evaporated.

Ahmad pulled her close. "I'm sorry, baby," he said. "I remember... I just hate texting. I'm always hitting the wrong key. But I'll try harder for you." His deep gentle tones were like a warm shower, soothing the pains in her chest. His strong arms were her sanctuary, her nomadic home.

In the safety of his arms, she allowed herself to remember too. The one she changed herself for, becoming the girl he preferred her to be. The one she mistook for her soulmate, worth sacrificing her own passions for. The one who ghosted her without explanation and tore her to pieces so deep it reached her spirit and shook her faith. In the safety of Ahmad's arms, she let the tears fall.

*Ping!*

Zakia shifted in the half-empty bed. She fished under the covers then between the pillows for her phone. She glanced at the display—a reminder she'd set for 6:00 am. A swipe revealed the contents.

*Do not message babe, just for seven days. Make him miss you. You can do it! The reward will be worth the torture. Bismillah...*

She stared. Seven days. Seven freakin' long days. Well, she was at work for four this week, so at least the seven to eight hours of distraction, selling loose-leaf-tea to customers, would help. But the lunch breaks, the cold evenings in bed alone...

"Ugh!!" Zakia tossed her phone aside. Deep breaths, she reminded herself. Keep busy. Get back into reading.

It was only day two.

Was this even normal, not talking to your husband for two days? Should she ask Bianca? No... she didn't want her to think they were having problems, especially given Bianca's work with clients in domestic disputes. But were these even problems? Or was she overthinking things?

Zakia turned over. She needed to talk to someone.

Her eyes lit up. Stacey, her psychologist friend.

Zakia stared at the ceiling of her dark room.

She felt bad bugging her, using her, making her work for free on her problems... No, she thought, just five more days for God's sake! Was she still a teenager, needing attention every second? Keep busy, keep busy, keep busy.

Day three. No messages nor calls from him.

Need to google if this is normal, she thought. If not, she needed to bring this up.

Communication is the most important thing after all, right?

Zakia breathed in the fresh air as she began her routine morning walk. She loved starting her day in nature. She used to walk every day, even in winter when it rained and she needed an umbrella and at least three layers of clothing. But when she got sick one year, it killed the habit.

It felt good, moving her body regularly and thinking—even mumbling—to herself to clear her head. Sometimes she would become conscious of familiar faces starting the morning like her.

Zakia smiled at the sight of a girl around her age walking her huge black dog. She used to be terrified of dogs—something her mother instilled. But somewhere along the way, she learnt not to move. They might approach her with curiosity, but as long as she was still, they would go away.

Her heart pounded loudly, all the same, the nearer the pair got. Zakia nodded at the nameless neighbour and smiled. "Morning."

Her eyes brightened in reply. "Morning."

Zakia opened her mouth to comment on the weather but the girl had already glanced away. Zakia shrugged and looked around the small oval that had a perimeter of about a kilometre. She'd walked two laps and was halfway through her third. A wooden bench coaxed her over—a spot to seek relationship advice from Dr Google.

*My husband works away is it normal not to talk for days*, she typed and braced herself for the results.

*Should couples talk to each other every day?*

*What to do when your husband is ignoring you*

*How to make it work when your partner is always travelling*

Hmm, that last one looks good, she thought and opened the website. She skimmed through the headings on the page.

*Talk it out beforehand*

*Don't romanticise your partner's life*

*Make time to talk every single day*

Zakia groaned loudly. "No!" She did not need this right now. What a stupid idea. What did Google know anyway? No relationship was the same, right? Should she talk to someone?

"Oh, Allah, guide me," she murmured under her breath.

Zakia looked up at the wide expanse of green. The rustle of leaves reverberated around her. The grass looked brown in the summer, but today, the green lawn glistened from the morning dew, coaxing her to tread it once again. A twitter of birds above her head was the only invitation she needed.

"Assalamu Alaikum Warahmatullah. Assalamu Alaikum Warahmatullah."

After the couplet of peace to each shoulder, Zakia turned and looked straight ahead. She uncrossed her legs and sat on her knees. She heard her phone buzz on her dresser table but trapped her hands in her armpits. She chanted God's praises over and over, before silently praying, "Yaa Haleem, please give me clarity and ease."

Al-Haleem—The Clement. It was her favourite name of God to call on. She recalled hearing an Islamic talk about praying to God and the mistake people make, asking God for patience through trials and tribulations. "When you ask God for patience, the time you need to exercise patience is through the difficult times. So, it's like asking God for more tough times! Instead, we should ask God for ease and call on His Mercy and Clemency."

It was an eye-opener.

Zakia folded the Sajadah and her prayer clothes, storing them neatly in one of those Ikea removable drawers.

When do I start tomorrow? she wondered as she headed to her dresser. It would be Christmas soon, the foot traffic already picking up at Garden City Shopping Centre. Boy did she need activity, some routine to take her mind off Ahmad. "What did you do on the long weekend?" she could predict her colleagues asking.

"Oh, you know, turned into a teenager again, getting mad at my husband. Tried to give him the silent treatment but, bloody hell, he doesn't seem to even notice!"

"He works over the weekend? A long weekend?" She would explain the life of a FIFO. They would ask if it's hard, is the money worth it.

"Zakia, what are you doing?" she asked herself. If her colleagues could see her now, staring at the wall above her dressing table for like half an hour, they would put her into a mental asylum. "What was I doing again?" She scratched her head. "My phone, duh."

Zakia's eyes widened at the sight of Ahmad's pet name on the display. A text message. Finally! Almost at the close of day three.

A sinking feeling... Why, oh why, was there always a sinking feeling when a silence was broken? Even after a year of blissful marriage, even with the white gold band and single diamond on her ring finger, why did she have this sick feeling? Why were these voices in her head saying, "He's sick of you now. You're too much for him. The time away has made him realise he doesn't want to be with you anymore."

The voices in her head that attempted to explain the unbearable silence her ex left her with...

Zakia clutched her phone until the pain brought her back to reality. Ahmad isn't *him*, she reminded herself as she opened the text.

*Babe I miss you.*

Zakia let out the breath she'd been holding. Her eyes pooled with relief. How could four words impact her so much?

Her thumbs flew across the screen, typing her essay of a reply. Many iterations of how she missed him, how hard it had been, the things she had got up to.

*Sorry work disaster. Let's video chat tonight.* Ahmad added.

She probed for more info.

*I'll tell you tonight habibti. It's killing me not seeing your beautiful face and hearing your voice. Oh, wear that red dress I love ;)*

Zakia chuckled then her heart expanded. *Okay my love.* She replied. *Also, thank you Ahmad. I know you hate texting. I really appreciate you making the effort. It makes me so happy.*

*Anything for you. You're worth it.*

After they confirmed a time, Zakia switched to her spreadsheets app that synced with the documents on her computer. She filled in the blanks with glee.

*End Date: Sun 19 September*

*Period (days): 3*

*Results: Ahmad messaged that he missed me & wants to video chat. Explained there was a work disaster. He could've messaged earlier explaining the work thing but I guess he might've been too stressed, only thinking about how to fix the crisis?*

*Conclusion: My worries were completely unfounded, but this spreadsheet really helped stop me from overwhelming Ahmad with unnecessary impatient messages.*

Zakia tapped on a new row.

*Hypothesis: He misses me like crazy if he hasn't heard from me for more than three days*

*Action: For another week, I will test this theory and patiently wait for him to initiate contact*

# Worthy

I groan out loud. It's got to be somewhere. I check the date on my watch. Five days left until Bianca's garden party. Will that be enough time? I should've checked the Officeworks website... I'll call them today.

"Ahmad, can you help me please!"

A few minutes pass. "Babe!!"

"Sorry, I was in the middle of something," Ahmad says as he enters our storage room. "What you looking for?"

"My old photo album from uni. It's Bianca's birthday on the tenth. I want to surprise her with a personalised card."

Ahmad squeezes my shoulder. "My thoughtful wife," he says before crouching down next to me. "What does it look like?"

"Not sure... I just remember it was with similar keepsake stuff, so other albums or even loose photos I didn't get a chance to organise yet."

"Okay," Ahmad says and gets to work.

I cough from the neglect that's collected and formed a thin lining on box-number-five. "Oh, this must be it!"

"See, I must be good luck."

I chuckle and reward my hubby with a huge grin. Back to business. I take out one album at a time, checking the contents briskly. "Ahmad, hold these please."

He sits cross-legged and collects the rejects between his thighs. He flicks through the still moments of my past. "Aww, Zakia, is this you?"

I turn to see myself in a white dress with red flowers, pouting for the camera. I laugh. "Yes. Wow, I thought Mum kept my toddler photos."

"You're so adorable," Ahmad says, slipping the picture out of its plastic sleeve. "I have to show this to my mum."

I ignore the sound of Ahmad cooing over other photos, intent on my mission. Where is that damned picture? I open the sixth album and beam—UWA's iconic clock tower. "Alhamdulillah! It has to be in this one."

"You found it?" Ahmad asks.

I flick through the pages. "I... think... yes!" Triumphant, I show Ahmad the first picture of Bianca and me together. I'm wearing a brown patterned scarf, matching brown top and black skirt while Bianca is adorned in the bright colours that exude her personality. About to separate the picture from its home, my eyes catch a familiar blue notebook, its jacket cracked and worn. My heart stops.

"What's wrong, habibti?"

My voice falters despite Ahmad's endearing address. I clear my throat. "My old notebook... from uni..."

"And?" Ahmad asks gently as he moves closer, touching my arm.

I take a deep breath. "I wrote about... *him*..." The one whose name I still can't say out loud.

Ahmad stiffens. "Oh." After a pause, he frowns. "You've brought him up before. Do you still have feelings for him?"

"No!" I respond immediately. "Not at all, babe," I say in a softened tone, smoothing away the creases between his dark brows. "It's just... what he did, it's like unfinished business."

"So, he's always going to be the third wheel in our marriage?"

I go quiet, looking at the frustration and hurt in my husband's eyes. I don't know how to respond, remembering the spreadsheet I'd started to track how long it took before Ahmad initiated contact—to cope with the times he didn't respond immediately to my messages. I gulp back tears.

Ahmad softens, lifts my chin so I'm looking at him eye-to-eye. "Zakia," he begins in a loving tone, "you need to stop giving him power over you like this. It's in the past. Keep it there and stop giving him power over your future."

My eyes sting. I sigh. "I know..." But how do I get over this? It's been, what, over a decade now but how do I move past this? Oh, Allah, guide me. Give me clarity and ease.

A memory prods—someone giving me advice. I can't remember who but their words replay in my mind with a renewed certainty.

*"The way to get over an emotion isn't to ignore it but to acknowledge it, listen to it, sit with it. Only then will it allow you to let it go."*

Ahmad's voice interrupts. "You okay?"

I force myself to take out the book before responding, "Yes... Habibi, can you hold me a moment?" I ask. "I think I'm going to burn my journal... But I want to re-read some of my old entries—"

"But why?" Ahmad interjects. "Why not just burn it? Why relive the pain?"

"Because the pain is here," I say, placing a hand on my heart. "And it keeps coming back from here," I add, touching my head. "I need to read the real events as I wrote them, as they happened. Because maybe my memory of them is warped by now and exaggerated."

Ahmad hesitates. "Okay, I trust you know what's best," he finally says, turning me and pulling my back against his broad chest.

I take a deep breath and open the journal cover. I flick through the pages, scanning the dates in search of April. I remember the month I met him clearly. Uni normally began in March, but I was still finding my feet. It wasn't until the month after that I started getting into the uni clubs.

I find the entry easily. My opening lines make it obvious.

*April 11*

*Arrrgh, the most exciting thing happened today! I met a guy!! Rather, I met the most amazing guy, who doesn't know I exist yet, maybe ever, but wow... He's got a slim build, wavy black hair, but his eyes... Seriously, his green eyes are to die for!*

*Okay, let me recap the details of how I met my dream husband. I finally joined that Islamic Halaqah that Hafsa had been telling me about. The topic being discussed was the Story of Nabi Musa. It so happened that he was leading the Halaqah today. Did I mention his voice? His voice, the command and confidence in it as he spoke, seriously makes me melt, made me tongue-tied.*

I pause a moment, a surreal feeling overcoming me. I can picture myself vividly, the naive excitement on my face. I place a hand over Ahmad's who is rubbing my thigh absentmindedly. "It's weird," I say. "It's like I'm reading about someone else... but someone I know deeply."

"But you're feeling okay?"

"So far, yes. I don't know what I was expecting but... Alhamdulillah, I'm feeling okay."

"Alhamdulillah," Ahmad says, squeezing me between his arms for a second.

I skip over a few passages that detail the topic discussed during that Islamic study circle and continue.

*Sigh... Oh Allah, I've never felt like this about anyone before. What I would give to have him like me too... I know he wouldn't notice someone like me, let alone develop feelings for me. Because I know I'm not good enough for him. But I'm ready to change. Oh*

*Allah, I pray from the bottom of my heart that one day I can be worthy of him.*

"Zakia, you alright?" Ahmad's voice pulls me back into my present moment.

I become conscious that my knuckles are hurting from clutching the book. I loosen my grip but my teeth remain clenched. "No," I say slowly. *Worthy of him*, I re-read. *Worthy...* of the heartache and scars he left when he stopped taking my calls, responding to my messages, and completely out of the blue, without any explanation? Ahmad is now a victim of the damage *he* caused too!

"Babe?" Ahmad turns me to face his concerned expression. "What is it?"

"I'm angry," I say calmly. "With myself... I just read that after I met him, I actually prayed asking Allah to make me *worthy* of him."

Ahmad scoffs. "Really?"

"Yes! I had such low self-esteem back then. But Alhamdulillah, this is the first time it's hit me, he wasn't worthy of *me*. But he was my first love. I was so attached to him thinking he was my soulmate. I don't think I would've ever left him even though I can see now how wrong he was for me." I pause and turn my gaze into space. "I'm realising now that in Allah's Mercy, it had to end one way or another for my own sake, so if I would never be the one to break things off..."

I sit for a moment with this thought. An immense feeling of gratitude overcomes me. Allah saved me, knowing every possible future and the greater pain I would've lived through had I married him. Allah knows me better than I know myself, knew that one day Ahmad would come into my life.

I turn back to my real soulmate, touch his face, trace the edges of his neatly trimmed beard. This beautiful man, secure in himself who I can talk to without filters—perhaps so patient and understanding because of his own flawed past. The unexpected beauty of it, how his imperfections have helped me be whole again.

"I always told you he didn't know your worth," Ahmad says.

I beam. "Yes, you're definitely right about that. But it's more than that," I say. "I deserved better." I plant a kiss on his nose. "I deserved this, us, *you*."

Ahmad crushes me between his arms. "I love you," he murmurs into my hair before taking my lips into his.

To follow the author's writing journey, stay up to date by joining Rai's Insiders:
www.raihanaty.com/join

# Glossary

**Al-Haleem**: "The Most Clement" in Arabic (one of the names of God.)

**Alhamdulillah**: "Praise be to God" in Arabic.

**Allah**: "The One God" in Arabic.

**Allahu Akbar**: "God is the Greatest" in Arabic.

**Assalamu Alaikum**: "Peace be upon you" in Arabic (a greeting used by Muslims.)

**Assalamu Alaikum Warahmatullah**: "Peace be upon you and God's mercy" in Arabic (an even better greeting used by Muslims and in their ritual prayers.)

**Eid**: "Feast, festival or holiday" in Arabic (a worldwide festival and celebration for Muslims.)

**Habibi**: "My love" in Arabic (used when addressing a male.)

**Habibti**: "My love" in Arabic (used when addressing a female.)

**Hijab**: The head covering and modest attire worn in public by some Muslim women.

**Jalsah**: "Sitting" in Arabic (refers to the sitting posture in the ritual prayer of Muslims.)

**Ka'bah**: "Cube" in Arabic (refers to the black square building draped in a silk and cotton veil, located in Makkah, Saudi Arabia, where Muslims perform a pilgrimage at least once in their life.)

**Mabrook**: "Congratulations" in Arabic.

**Nikah**: A religious ceremony for a Muslim couple to be legally wed under Islamic law.

**Qiyam**: "Standing" in Arabic (refers to the standing posture in the ritual prayer of Muslims.)

**Ruku'**: "Bowing" in Arabic (refers to the belt-low bowing posture in the ritual prayer of Muslims.)

**Sadaqah**: "Righteousness" in Arabic (refers to the voluntary giving of charity.)

**Sajadah**: A small rug used by Muslims during their ritual prayers.

**Sajdah**: "Prostration" in Arabic (refers to the low-bowing posture or prostration in the ritual prayer of Muslims.)

**Salah**: "Prayer" in Arabic (refers to the ritual prayer of Muslims performed five times a day.)

**Salam**: "Peace" in Arabic (sometimes used as an abbreviation of the full greeting "Assalamu Alaikum".)

**Wa Alaikum Salam**: "And unto you peace" in Arabic (the usual response to the greeting "Assalamu Alaikum" used by Muslims.)

**Wudhu**: the ritual washing or ablution to be performed in preparation for the ritual prayer of Muslims.

**Yaa Haleem**: "Oh the Most Clement" in Arabic (used when calling on the name of God that represents His clemency.)

# Acknowledgments

I wrote the first draft of this collection during a Centre for Stories fellowship in 2019. And so I must begin by thanking this precious place for being so integral to my growth as a writer. What path I may have ended up on had I not discovered its "Write Night" back in 2017, which has resulted in so many incredible opportunities that have shaped me into the writer I am today.

To all the wonderful people I met at the Centre for Stories Write Nights, in particular Emily Paull, Belinda Hermawan and Chris Karsten; the safe space you created to write without interruptions and with no pressure to share, the inspiration I garnered from the diverse projects in the room, from novels to stand-up comedy routines, and just the warmth and welcome.

To all the members of the various writing groups I've been part of, in particular, Inklings Writers' Workshop and World Writers Perth. I've learnt so much and become a better writer, not only from our formal workshops, but from hearing everyone's amazing work.

To Elizabeth Tan, who I was blessed to have been paired with during a Centre for Stories writing mentorship. Your humbleness despite your immense knowledge and gifts, but especially your gentleness throughout the editing process helped ease my anxiety over sharing my writing with others and getting constructive feedback.

To Emily Paull; you are too special to only mention once. Thank you for helping me edit these stories, for your honesty and fresh perspectives. This collection is so much more complete thanks to you.

Dearest MM; my best friend and most passionate fan of everything I do. Your infectious excitement for my writing has helped me in times of doubt and uncertainty.

To my beta readers, Natasha Aburman, Louise Allan, Fiona Robertson & Melinda Tognini. I appreciate your time, your constructive input, but especially your warm encouraging words that gave me the confidence to persist in sharing these stories with the world.

To the rest of the 5 am, turned 6 am, then eventually 7 am writers crew; Jess Gately, Michael Trant, Holden Sheppard, Raphael Farmer, Alicia Tuckerman, Jen Bowman, Rebecca Freeman, Samantha House and Lana Pecherczyk. Despite my inactivity in the chat, just know that your friendship, your enthusiasm and hearing of your own highs and lows have made me feel less alone in this otherwise solitary profession.

Finally, to my family, both by blood and by choice, whose names need no mention because you already know the huge space you occupy in my heart. Your love and support, both spoken and unspoken, are deeply cherished.